Great Inventions

CONTENTS

CREATIVE EDUCATION

Great Inventions

People have been inventing things to make their lives easier since man first appeared on the scene almost half a million years ago. Some inventions, such as the wheel, proved to be so useful that they changed people's lives forever. Others were so silly they disappeared without a trace!

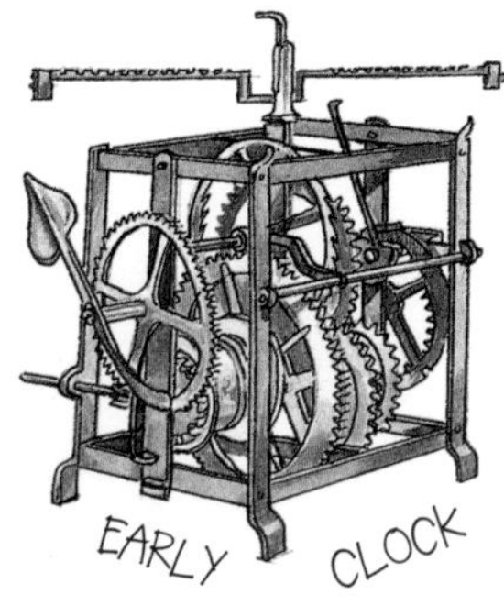

Wheels in motion
Wheels were first used for transport more than 5,000 years ago. Later, they were adapted for use as water wheels, windmills, spinning wheels, and pulleys, as well as cogs and gears in clocks and machinery.

All steamed up
Early steam engines, like Thomas Newcomen's engine of 1712, were designed to pump water out of mines. But steam engines soon changed the course of history when they were turned to powering factory machines.

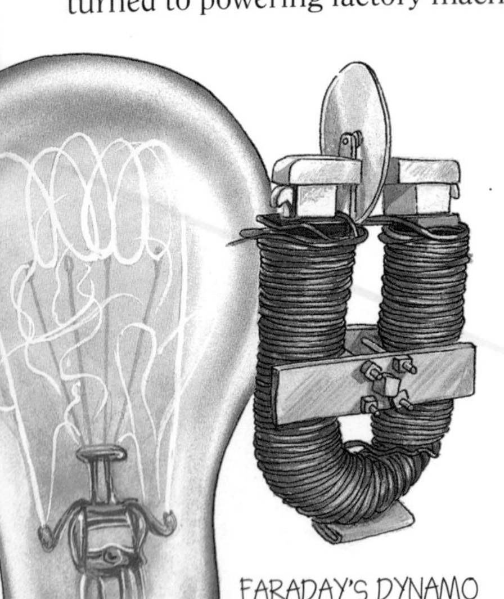

The father of electricity
Michael Faraday is known as the "Father of Electricity" because, in 1831, he invented the first electricity generator, called a dynamo. The modern generators that produce much of our electricity, supplying our homes with light, heat, and power, are driven by steam.

Power to the motor car
The invention of the internal-combustion engine in 1860 led to the birth of the automobile. Most modern car engines are based on this 4-stroke engine built by Nikolaus Otto in 1876.

A new dawn
The computer age began with the invention of the silicon chip. By the 1970s, the workings of a computer could be placed on a few chips the size of ladybugs.

Close-up of electric circuits on a silicon chip.

. . . And some not so great!

- One invention that never quite made it was a machine for walking on water. Riders were supported on floats and moved by turning paddles attached to their feet.
- A device for getting people up in the morning tipped the bed up and plummeted the sleeping occupant into a bath full of cold water.

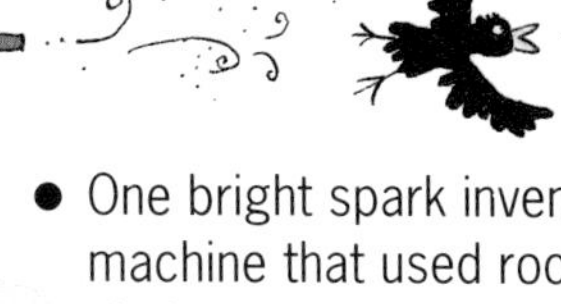

- One bright spark invented a machine that used rocking-chair power to churn butter and rock the baby at the same time!

Steaming Ahead

Until the invention of the steam engine, machines were powered by people, animals, or water wheels. The coming of steam helped to create a boom in industry—called the Industrial Revolution—and resulted in new forms of transport.

HERO'S STEAM MACHINE

Blowing steam
The first steam machine was built in about A.D. 100 by an Egyptian named Hero of Alexander. But it didn't have any practical use.

Turning up the steam
In 1784 James Watt built a powerful new steam engine that could convert up and down motion into circular, or rotary, motion. Soon his engines were powering cotton mills and iron foundries all over Britain.

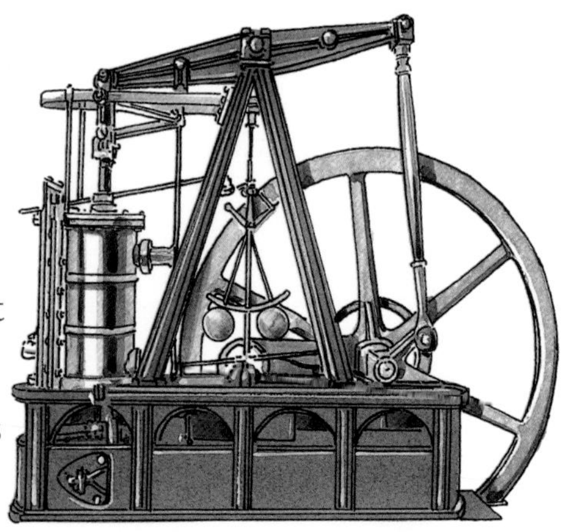

WATT'S ROTARY STEAM ENGINE

Catch Me Who Can
The first person to put a steam engine on rails and turn it into a locomotive was Richard Trevithick, in 1803. Five years later he took another locomotive—*Catch Me Who Can*—to London, where he carried brave passengers around a circular track at 5 mph (8kmh).

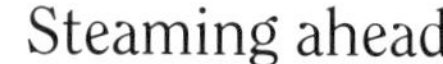

Going like a rocket
George Stephenson's *Rocket* locomotive of 1829 was the first vehicle to travel faster than a horse, reaching speeds of 35 mph (56kmh).

William Huskisson became the first person to be killed by a train when he was hit by the Rocket *on its first day of service.*

Horse power – San Francisco style

In San Francisco in the 1870s, steam street cars were creating havoc in the streets, scaring all the horses. So one Mr. Mathewson had the bright idea of building a horse-shaped street car. Luckily, it seemed to do the trick!

Steam on the road
Trains weren't the only vehicles to use steam. Nicolas Cugnot built this steam tractor in 1770, but he drove it into a wall on its first day out! A few years later, steam was also being used to power ships (see page 8).

On the Road

After the invention of the steam engine, there were many attempts to build a steam-powered road vehicle. But steam engines were too heavy to be practical. Then the internal-combustion engine was invented, and the first cars soon followed.

1885 BENZ

The first car
Built by Karl Benz in 1885, the first automobile looked more like a tricycle. It was steered with a tiller and reached 9 mph (15kmh).

On all fours
Gottlieb Daimler fitted a petrol engine to an ordinary horse-drawn carriage in 1886 and invented the first 4-wheel automobile.

Danger ahead!

In Britain, in the early days of motoring, someone had to walk ahead of the car waving a red flag to warn other road users of its approach.

The Tin Lizzie
To begin with, cars were an expensive luxury. Then, in 1908, Henry Ford started mass-producing his Model T Ford. Nicknamed the Tin Lizzie, it was the first cheap and reliable automobile.

Rolling along

Richard Hemmings designed this Flying Yankee unicycle in 1869, eight years after the first pedal bicycles were built. Bicycles weren't allowed on the roads until 1888, and even then riders had to ring their bells continually.

Rolling along

- While Benz was building the first car, Gottlieb Daimler and Wilhelm Maybach were building the first motorbike. It had a wooden frame and small wheels at the back to keep it upright.
- Early bicycles, such as the Draisine of 1817, had no pedals and were propelled by the rider's feet.

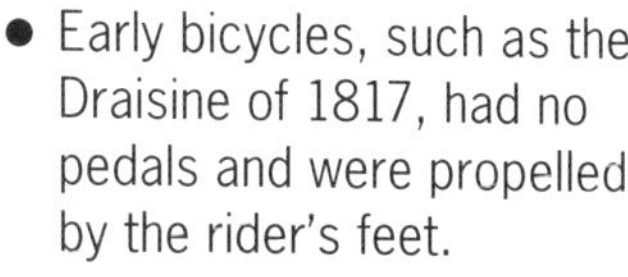

- John Dunlop made one of the first pneumatic (air-filled) tires in 1888 for his son's tricycle. They weren't used on cars until 1895.

Power from the sun

Today, pollution caused by the internal-combustion engine has become a major problem. So some people have built cars that are powered by the Sun. Called the Sunraycer, this solar car won the first solar-powered car race in Australia in 1987.

All at Sea

Early boats were propelled through the water using sticks or paddles. But by 4000 B.C., people had discovered that a square of fabric could be used to catch the wind and make the boat go faster—they had invented the sail.

EGYPTIAN SHIP, 1500 B.C.

Setting sail

The ancient Egyptians built the first sailing ships, with one square sail on a single mast. Their ships still needed oars, in case the wind dropped.

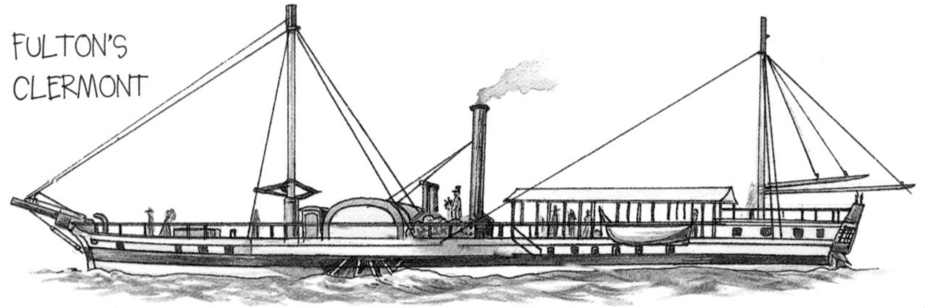

Breathing flames and smoke

Robert Fulton's paddle steamer *Clermont* was one of the first steamships. Built in 1807, it was said to be like "a monster moving through the water, breathing flames and smoke."

Ship of doom

In 1845, Isambard Kingdom Brunel's *Great Britain* became the first iron steamship to cross the Atlantic. His next ship, the *Great Eastern*, didn't do so well. She was launched only after two failed attempts, during which one man died. Then an explosion on board killed six more. She became damaged in a storm and finally hit a rock outside New York harbor.

War underwater

One of the first submarines was the *Hunley*, built during the American Civil War. It sank its first target but, alas, went down as well.

The Hunley was built out of an old boiler and was powered by eight men turning a crank.

Swinging time

Henry Bessemer suffered from seasickness, so he designed the perfect cure—a ship with a swinging saloon that always stayed upright. But his new invention rolled so violently that it made people even more sick, and the saloon had to be bolted down.

The unsinkable traveling case

In the 1880s, one ingenious inventor designed a suitcase that doubled as a life jacket in times of need.

Floating on air

In 1954, Christopher Cockerell reversed the engine on a vacuum cleaner, so that it blew air instead of sucking it, and used it to help him design his new invention—the hovercraft.

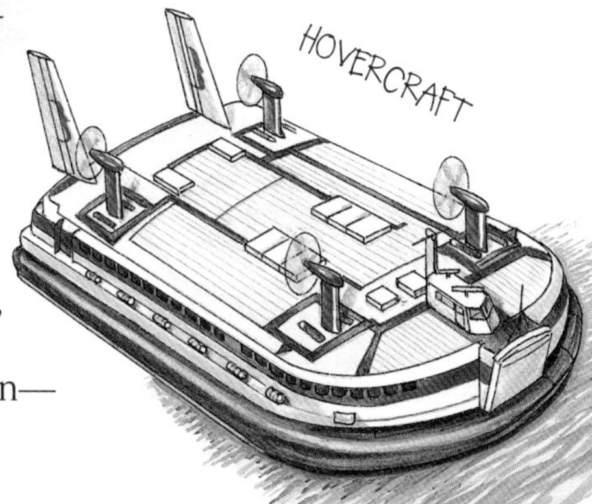

Up, Up, and Away

People had always dreamed of being able to fly, but it was not until hot air balloons were invented in the 18th century that the dream became a reality.

Flights of fantasy
As well as being one of the world's greatest painters, Leonardo da Vinci was also an inventor, whose notebooks contain sketches of amazing devices such as this flying machine.

LEONARDO DA VINCI

Flying high
In 1783, the Montgolfier brothers demonstrated the first passenger-carrying hot air balloon. It stayed aloft for eight minutes before making a safe landing, much to the relief of its three passengers—a goat, a duck, and a cock!

Is it a bird? Is it a plane?

Crazy crafts

The 19th-century obsession with building a machine that could fly resulted in some weird designs, such as this 8-eagle-powered device. Of course, it never flew!

Seven propellers driven by foot pedals, hand cranks, and a motor couldn't get this craft off the ground.

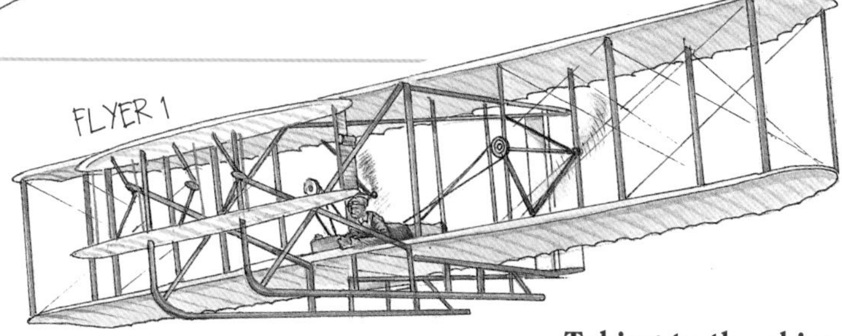

Taking to the skies

The first people to make a successful powered flight were brothers Wilbur and Orville Wright. One day in 1903 they made four flights in their *Flyer I* biplane, the fourth lasting 59 seconds and covering 852 ft. (260m).

Flying firsts

- British engineer Frank Whittle demonstrated the first jet aircraft engine in 1937. But the Germans built the first jet aircraft—the *Heinkel 178*—in 1939, beating the British by two years.
- The first supersonic flight was in 1947. Chuck Yeager flew the *Bell XS–1* at Mach 1.015 (670 mph).
- Called the *Gyroplane*, the first successful helicopter made a record flight of more than one hour in 1936.

Blasting off

The first spacecraft to carry a person into space was the Russian *Vostok I*, in 1961. Twenty years later, the U.S. launched its first reusable spacecraft, the space shuttle *Columbia*.

Weapons of War

People have been designing more and more sophisticated weapons since the bow and arrow were invented 30,000 years ago. By A.D. 1000 the Chinese were using gunpowder for fireworks and sending signals.

Fire power
The ancient Greeks and Romans used catapults and ballistae to bombard the enemy with stones or a burning substance called "Greek fire."

Early cannons
Cannons were first used in Europe from about 1326. The earliest ones were very brittle and just as likely to explode in the user's face as to damage enemy defenses.

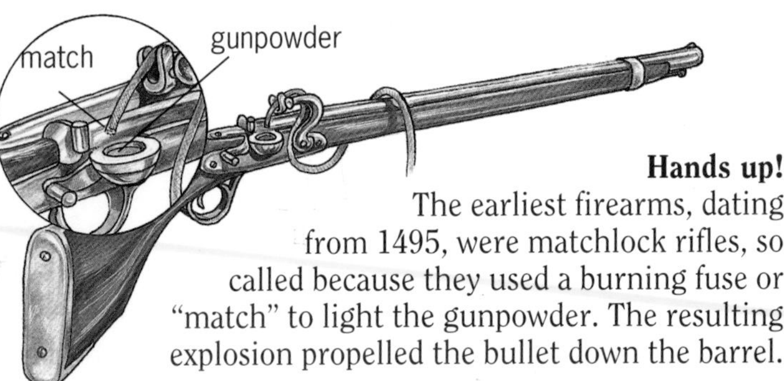

Hands up!
The earliest firearms, dating from 1495, were matchlock rifles, so called because they used a burning fuse or "match" to light the gunpowder. The resulting explosion propelled the bullet down the barrel.

Blow your head off

This strange device was invented by Albert Pratt in 1916. Wearers fired the gun built into their helmet by blowing on the mouthpiece, no doubt praying at the same time that it wouldn't blow their head off!

The British development of a tracked armored vehicle was so secret that the machine was referred to as a water carrier—or tank, for short—to disguise its true nature. The first successful model, demonstrated in January 1916, was called *Big Willie*.

Going out with a bang
Explosives manufacturer Alfred Nobel realized he had to make a more stable explosive when his factory blew up for the second time. In 1867 he invented dynamite.

Rocket power
Germany's secret weapon during World War II was the V–2 rocket, the first of many guided missiles. The V stood for "vergeltung," meaning vengeance.

Death and destruction
The most destructive weapon ever used was the atom bomb. Two were dropped on Japan in 1945, killing more than 150,000 people.

Medical Inventions

Up until the late 18th century, doctors' most valued tools were their saws, scalpels, and leeches. But all that changed in the 19th century when a host of discoveries and inventions transformed medical practices.

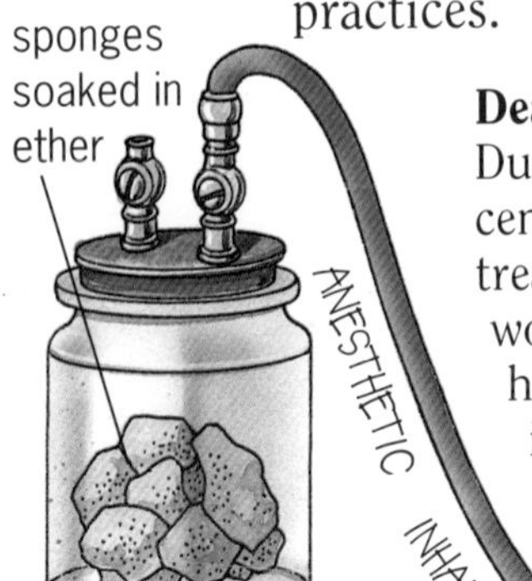

Death masks
During the 17th century, doctors treating plague victims sometimes wore these strange masks with herb-filled beaks to guard against infection. What they didn't realize was that the infection was caused by flea bites, so the masks were useless!

Laughing at pain
People inhaled laughing gas and ether just for fun until dentist Robert Morton recognized their pain-killing effects in 1846. Soon he was using these "anesthetics" to perform painless surgery.

Don't be shy
In 1816, shy Dr. René Laënnec used a rolled-up piece of paper to listen to a female patient's chest. He had just invented the first stethoscope!

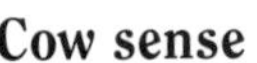

Cow sense
Edward Jenner performed the first vaccination in 1796, using a mild form of cowpox to protect against small-pox. Cartoonists of the day imagined all of Jenner's patients turning into cows!

Medical firsts

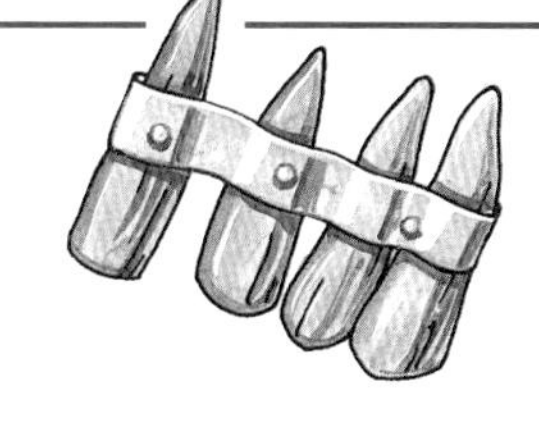

- The first false teeth date from 700 B.C. They were carved from bone and held with a gold band.
- The first spectacles were made in Italy in 1287. They were used for reading.
- The hypodermic syringe was invented by Charles Pravaz in 1853.
- Aspirins were first made in the 1890s. Now, 123 billion are swallowed worldwide every year.

X marks the spot
In 1895, Wilhelm Röntgen discovered a new kind of ray that he used to take a photograph of the bones inside his wife's hand. He called his find X ray—X standing for unknown. Using special machines, doctors were soon taking X rays of people's bodies to diagnose broken bones and various illnesses.

When X rays were first discovered, people had fun imagining what life would be like with X-ray vision.

Razor-sharp light
Lasers were first invented in 1960 for use in industry. Now they are also used in surgery for cutting through flesh—they can even be used to remove tattoos!

Instruments of Science

The quest for scientific knowledge has resulted in a wealth of ingenious inventions, some designed for observation, others for measurement or navigation, and many for proving scientific theory.

GALILEO AT HIS TELESCOPE

On trial for life

The first person to use a telescope to observe the planets was Italian scientist Galileo Galilei in 1609. He believed that Earth revolved around the Sun, but the church (incorrectly) thought otherwise, and sentenced him to death. He was spared his life only when he admitted he was wrong.

A world in miniature

When Robert Hooke built one of the first microscopes in the 1660s, he was able to observe tiny creatures, such as fleas and lice, in detail for the first time.

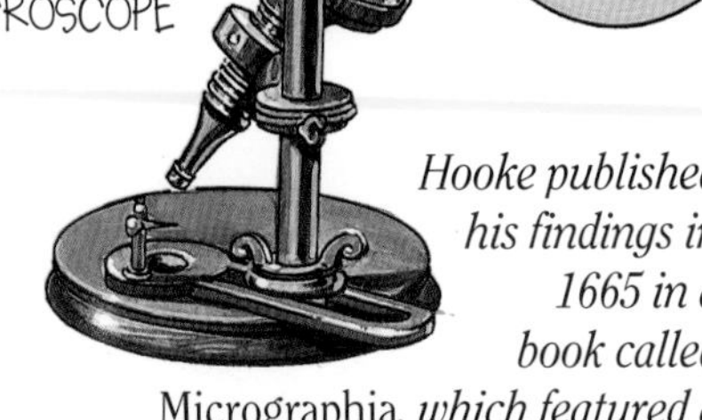

Hooke published his findings in 1665 in a book called Micrographia, *which featured a 2 ft. (60cm) long drawing of a flea.*

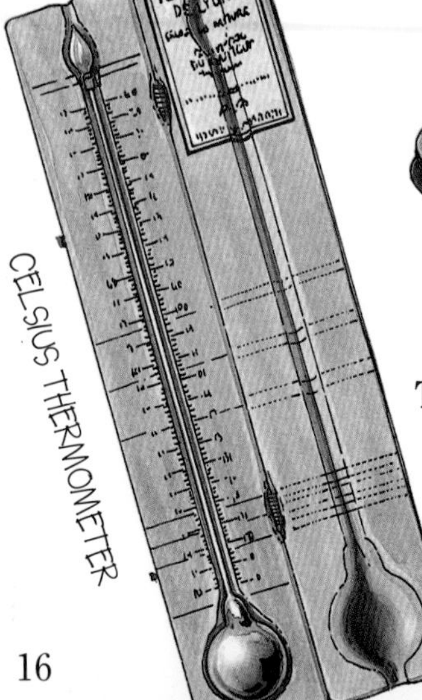

Taking the temperature

Galileo invented a thermometer in 1592. But it was astronomer Anders Celsius who, in 1742, introduced the centigrade scale still used today.

Shocking entertainment
One 18th-century inventor entertained his friends in a most unusual way. Using this strange apparatus, he was able to generate electricity that he then passed down a gentleman's sword into a spoonful of alcohol held by a brave lady. The resulting spark made the alcohol burst into flames.

On the high seas
Sailors had long navigated using the stars. Then, in 1731, John Hadley invented the octant, for measuring latitude—the angle between the horizon and the Sun. This enabled navigators to pinpoint their positions much more accurately.

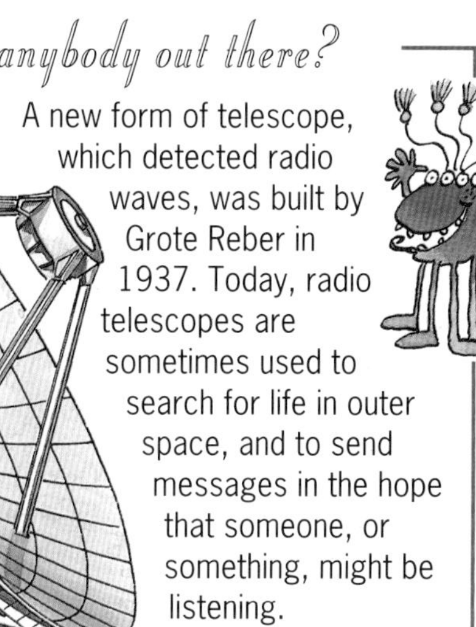

Is anybody out there?

A new form of telescope, which detected radio waves, was built by Grote Reber in 1937. Today, radio telescopes are sometimes used to search for life in outer space, and to send messages in the hope that someone, or something, might be listening.

Clocks, Calculators, ...

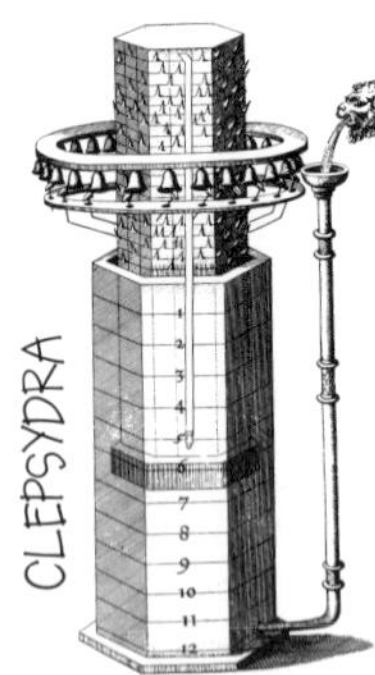

Early methods for calculating time relied on the Sun, water, or sand. Then, in A.D. 1300, the first mechanical clocks were made. Machines for mathematical calculations were invented 300 years later.

As time goes by
The Greek inventor Ctesibius designed this water clock in 300 B.C. It is called a clepsydra.

Swinging pendulums
Early mechanical clocks were not very accurate and had no minute hands. Then Christiaan Huygens built the first pendulum clock in 1656, which was accurate to five minutes a day.

HUYGENS' PENDULUM CLOCK

Simple sums
The abacus has been used for simple addition for the last 5,000 years.

ABACUS

Mechanical calculators
In 1642, 19-year-old Blaise Pascal invented a new type of calculating machine which, using a system of gears and wheels, was able to subtract as well as add.

PASCAL CALCULATOR

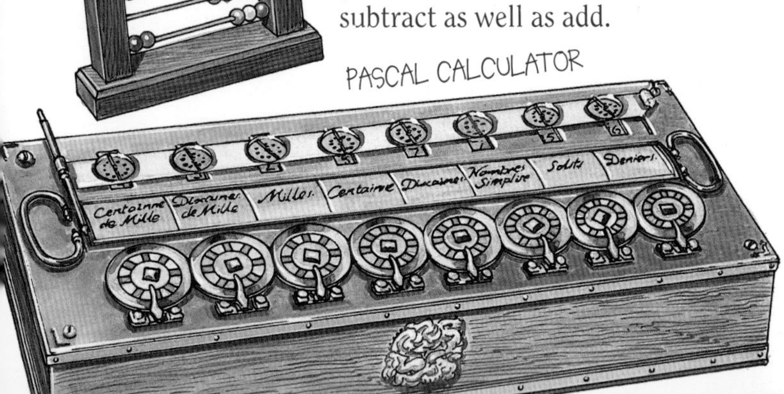

and Computers

The early days

Charles Babbage worked on a mechanical computing machine—his analytical engine (right)—for 37 years. When he died in 1871 he'd still only built a small part of it. Even so, he had designed the first computer.

The earliest electronic computer was ENIAC, built in 1946. Containing 18,000 valves and occupying several rooms, it could do 5,000 additions per second!

Computers for everyone

Steve Jobs and Steve Wozniak designed the first popular personal computer—the Apple II—in Jobs's parents' garage in 1976–77. Jobs had to sell his van, and Wozniak his expensive calculator, to fund the project. The Apple II was also the first computer able to generate color graphics.

Can this be happening to me?

Almost real

Wearing a special helmet that displays realistic scenes before their eyes, people are transported into an exciting world of make-believe. This is called virtual reality.

Machines at Work

New machines are constantly being invented to help people work faster and more efficiently on the farm, in the factory, and in the office.

Down on the farm
The first reaping machine, invented by Reverend Bell in 1826, lightened the farmer's load at harvest time.

Tractors at work
The first successful tractor was the Ivel tractor, built in 1902 by Dan Albone, also known as "Smiling Dan." Henry Ford started mass producing tractors in 1916.

Spinning at speed
Spinning wheels had been in use in Europe since about 1200. Then, in 1764, James Hargreaves invented the spinning jenny—a spinning machine that could spin eight threads at once, instead of just one.

Punch card patterns
Another advancement in weaving came in 1801, when Joseph Marie Jacquard invented a loom that could be programmed using punch cards to weave complex patterns.

What a riot!

When French tailor Barthélemy Thimonnier invented a sewing machine in about 1830, he caused a riot among Parisian tailors who, seeing his invention as a threat, stormed his shop and smashed all 80 of his machines.

Elias Howe invented his sewing machine in 1843. When Isaac Singer brought out a domestic sewing machine based on Howe's design in 1851, Howe sued and won $25,000 in royalties.

HOWE SEWING MACHINE

Keeping it slow

One of the first typewriters was this Glidden and Scholes model of 1873. While Christopher Scholes was designing it, the keys kept jamming. So he moved the most used keys as far apart as possible, which solved the problem but made the machine slower to use. We still use his "QWERTY" arrangement of keys today!

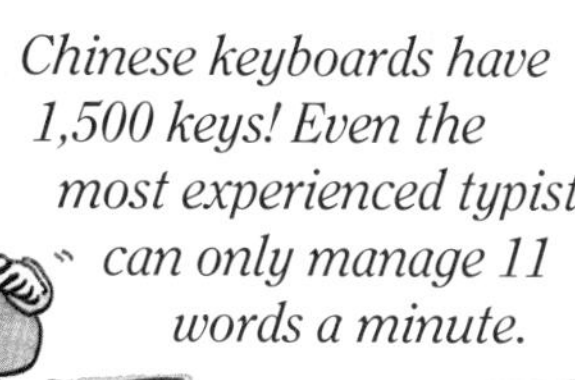

Chinese keyboards have 1,500 keys! Even the most experienced typist can only manage 11 words a minute.

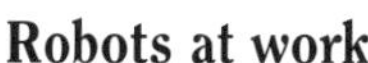

Robots at work

The first industrial robots were built in America in 1962. Now they are widely used, especially in the car industry where they do such jobs as welding and paint spraying.

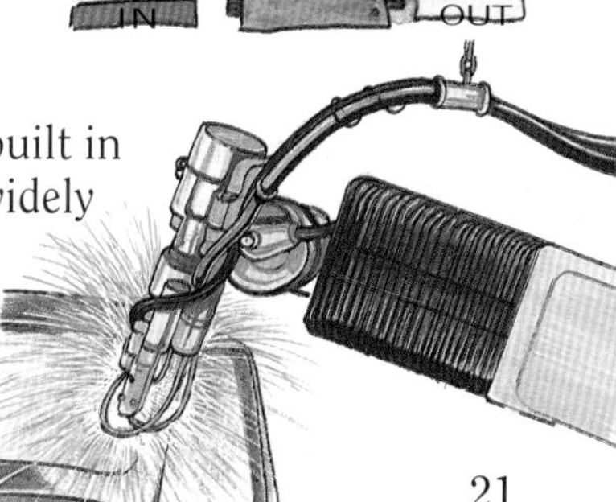

Building and Materials

A host of inventions and the development of new materials—cheap steel last century and plastics this—led to a revolution in the construction of buildings and homes.

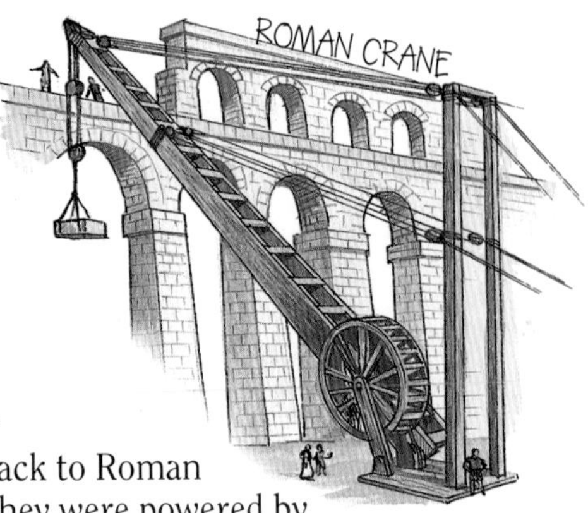

People power

Cranes date back to Roman times, when they were powered by slaves inside a treadmill.

BESSEMER CONVERTER

A steely strength

Although much stronger than iron, steel used to be expensive to make. Then, in 1856, Henry Bessemer invented a "converter" for making large quantities of cheap steel. Soon, steel was being used to form the skeletons of skyscrapers.

Going up!

Elevators did not become popular until 1854, when Elisha Otis demonstrated his new safety elevator by standing in it while someone cut the cable.

Thanks to elevators, it was practical to build above six stories. By 1885 the first sky-scraper had been built, in Chicago.

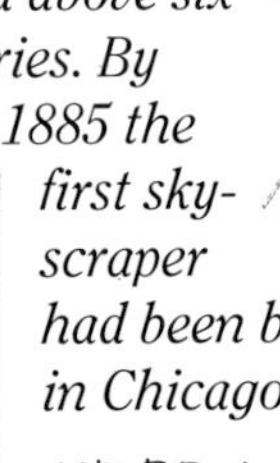

Royal flush
The first flushing toilet was built in 1589 by Elizabeth I of England's godson, John Harington. When the queen saw his impressive invention, she had one built for herself.

Let there be light
While Joseph Swan was inventing the electric lamp in Britain, Thomas Edison was doing the same thing in America. Edison's proved the more practical design, and in 1880 he started selling them to the general public at $2.50 each.

Material of a thousand uses

- Alexander Parkes invented the first plastic in 1862 out of mothballs and cotton pads.
- John Wesley invented a plastic in 1869 as a substitute for ivory in billiard balls. Called celluloid, it was later used to make film for movies.
- In 1907 Leo Baekeland described his new plastic—Bakelite—as a "material of a thousand uses." It was used, for example, for radios, clocks, and cameras.
- Wallace Carothers led a team in 1934 that designed an artificial silk called nylon. The first nylon stockings appeared in 1940.

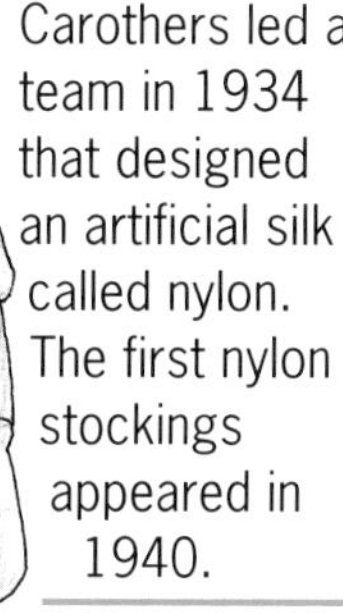

In the Home

1850s IRON

Many of the household items we take for granted were invented in the 19th and early 20th century. But some of these early designs look very different from the way they look today!

There must be an easier way than this!

Ironing away
This 1850s iron had burning charcoal inside and came complete with chimney and bellows! Electric irons were invented in 1882.

Can the can
Canned foods were first produced by Nicolas Appert in 1812. Can openers, alas, weren't invented until the 1860s, so people had to open their cans using a hammer and chisel.

BOOTH VACUUM CLEANER

The noisy serpent
After watching a demonstration of railroad carriage cleaners that *blew* the dust away, Hubert Booth decided to invent a cleaner that *sucked* up the dust instead. In 1901 he made the first powered vacuum cleaner. Described as a "noisy serpent," it was so big it had to be pulled by a horse, and stayed in the street while houses were cleaned using a long hose.

Zipping up
The zipper was invented by Whitcomb Judson in 1893. But it didn't live up to its trade name of C-Curity—it often came undone. The modern style of zipper was designed by Gideon Sundback in 1914.

JUDSON ZIPPER

Wash day blues

Washing machines were introduced in the 1840s. This sophisticated model from 1897 was hand-cranked and had a mangle. Alva Fisher designed the first electric washing machine in 1906.

Time to get up

Getting up in the morning was always a problem—until the invention of this teamaker in 1904! It worked using a system of levers, springs, and steam from the kettle.

Guess that gadget!

Here are some useful household items from the last century. Can you guess what they are? See below for answers.

(1) Glove stretchers for reshaping gloves after washing; (2) candle snuffer; (3) pleating iron; (4) hot water bottle; (5) sugar nippers for cutting small pieces off large blocks of sugar.

Keeping in Touch

People have been devising means of communicating with each other since fire and smoke signals were first used. Communication using pictures, and later symbols, developed into the first forms of writing more than 5,000 years ago.

Printing breakthrough
Johannes Gutenberg invented the printing press in about 1450 and first used it to print bibles. Each page was made up using individual metal letters. Then it was inked by hand and damp paper was pressed on top.

ROTARY PRESS, 1862

Printing progress
In 1845 Robert Hoe invented a rotary press, in which the type was arranged on one of two cylinders. This one could print six copies at once.

TELEGRAPH MACHINE, 1845

Long distance
Invented in 1837 by William Cooke and Charles Wheatstone, the electric telegraph was the first effective means of communicating over long distances. Electric signals were sent along wires to a receiver where they caused needles to point to letters, spelling out the message.

Tapping messages
In 1838, Samuel Morse invented a code that could be used to send messages by telegraph. The code was tapped out using a Morse key.

MORSE KEY

Morse code

A .-
B -...
C -.-.
D -..
E .
F ..-.
G --.
H ....
I ..
J .---
K -.-
L .-..
M --
N -.
O ---
P .--.
Q --.-
R .-.
S ...
T -
U ..-
V ...-
W .--
X -..-
Y -.--
Z --..

A cry for help

In 1876, Alexander Graham Bell was about to test his new invention—the telephone—when he spilled acid on his trousers. When he shouted to his assistant next door for help, "Mr. Watson, come here! I need you!" his words were transmitted down the telephone line, much to the surprise of both men.

The first telephone exchange was opened within a year of the telephone's invention. Above, Bell is seen opening the New York to Chicago telephone link in 1892.

Losing out

When insurance salesman Lewis Waterman lost a deal to his rival in 1884 because his pen spattered ink across the contract, he went away and invented the first practical fountain pen.

Picture from space

Today, satellites orbiting Earth are used to relay telephone calls and television pictures around the world. The first to transmit live TV shows was *Telstar*, launched by the U.S. in 1962.

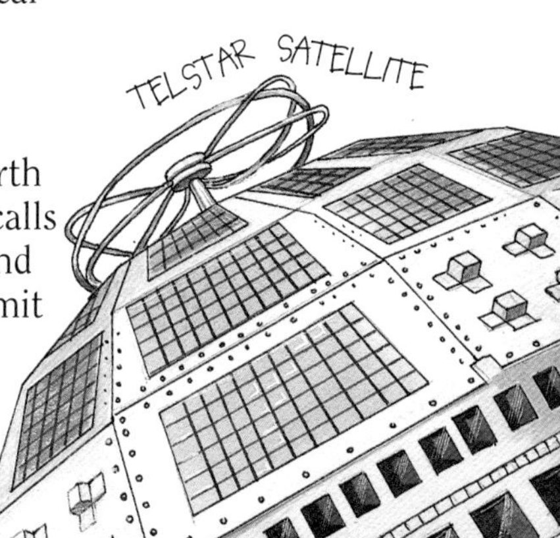

That's Entertainment

Before 1900, home entertainment consisted largely of sing-alongs around the piano or card games in the parlor! But all that was to change in the early years of the 20th century.

The birth of radio
In 1901, Guglielmo Marconi used radio waves to send a message across the Atlantic, without the use of wires. Soon, his "wireless telegraphy" was adapted to transmit voices and music, and radio was born.

1924 RADIO SET

Early radio sets had earphones instead of loud speakers to pick up the weak broadcasting signals.

Time for a drink
In the U.S. during Prohibition, when alcohol was banned, some radios were built with special hiding places for booze!

To catch a murderer

Wireless telegraphy caused a sensation in 1910 when it was used to catch wife-murderer Dr. Crippen. Crippen and his lady friend (disguised as a boy) were fleeing London on board an ocean liner when the captain became suspicious. So he wired Scotland Yard and the police were able to arrest Crippen.

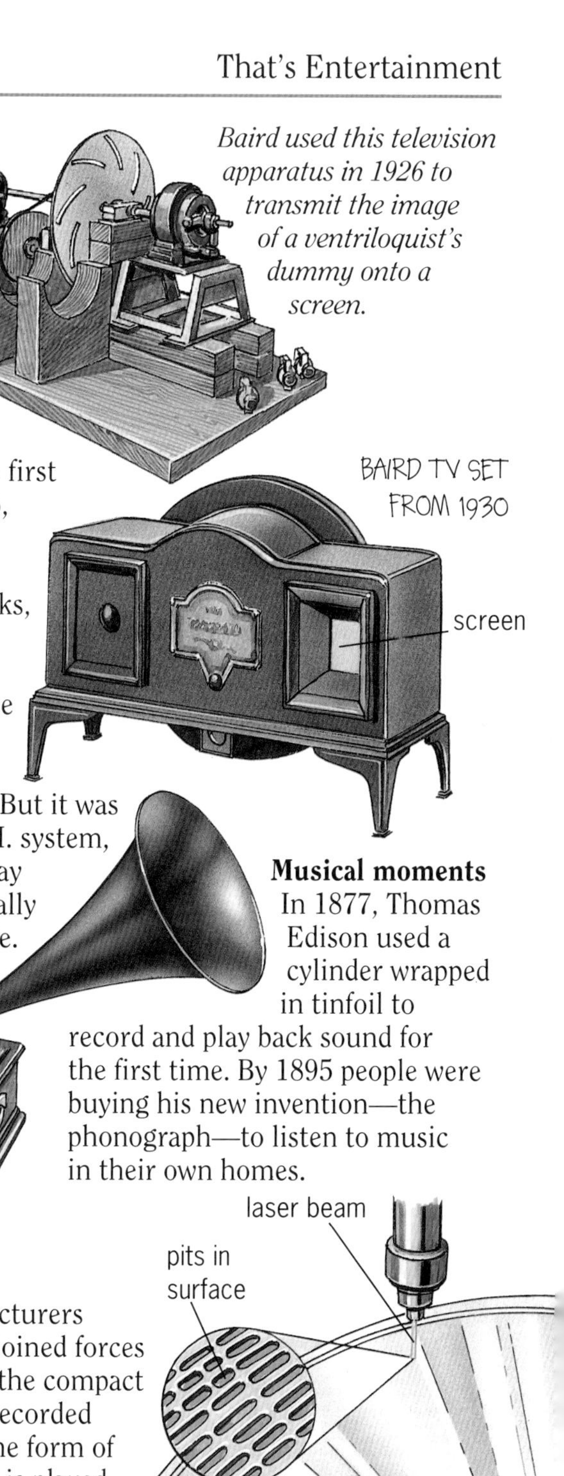

Baird used this television apparatus in 1926 to transmit the image of a ventriloquist's dummy onto a screen.

TV triumph
John Logie Baird demonstrated the first television in 1926, using a series of spinning disks, called Nipkow disks, to transmit an image onto a screen. By 1929 he had opened the world's first television studio. But it was the Marconi/E.M.I. system, using a cathode-ray tube, that was finally adopted worldwide.

Musical moments
In 1877, Thomas Edison used a cylinder wrapped in tinfoil to record and play back sound for the first time. By 1895 people were buying his new invention—the phonograph—to listen to music in their own homes.

CD takes a turn
Electrical manufacturers Philips and Sony joined forces in 1982 to invent the compact disc. Sounds are recorded onto the disk in the form of tiny pits. The disk is played back using a laser beam.

Photography and Film

The first known photograph was taken by Nicéphore Niépce as long ago as 1826. As photographic techniques improved, people turned their attention to making the pictures move, and movies were invented.

DAGUERRE CAMERA

Smile please!
In the 1830s, Louis Daguerre produced the first successful photographs, using metal plates. His "daguerreotypes" started a craze, and soon everybody wanted their portrait taken.

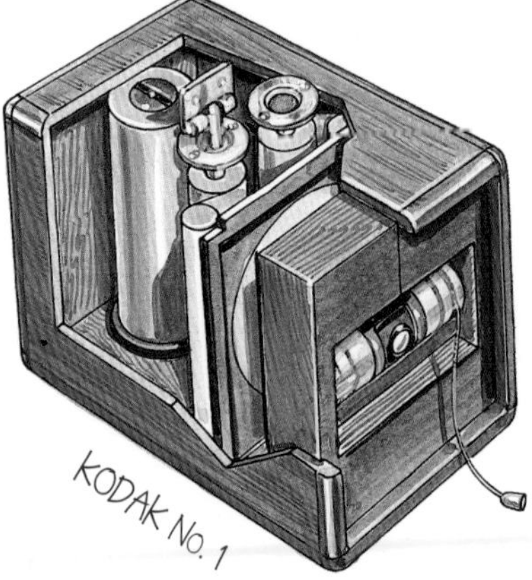

Happy snaps
At first, photography was for specialists, until George Eastman invented a camera for the "lazy, casual millions" in 1888. His Kodak No. 1 was the first camera to use roll film instead of plates.

ZOETROPE

Called a zoetrope, this toy was one of many 19th-century inventions designed to make pictures "move."

At a gallop
In 1872, in order to win a bet over whether a running horse ever has all feet off the ground at once, Eadweard Muybridge used a row of 24 cameras to take this sequence of photographs. Then he projected the photos onto a screen to re-create the movement.

Movie magic
Thomas Edison and William Dickson invented the first "moving picture" machine—called a kinetoscope—in 1888. Viewers watched the 20-second-long movie by putting a nickel in the slot and looking through the eyepiece at the top.

Cinema is born
In 1895, brothers Louis and Auguste Lumière put movies on to the "big screen" by inventing the cinématographe—a combined camera and projector.

- The first person to show movies on screen was Louis Le Prince in 1888. Alas, he boarded a train in 1890 and was never seen again!
- Emile Reynaud gave the first cartoon show in 1887 using pictures he had drawn himself.
- Early movie film was only sensitive to red light, so actors had to wear green makeup to make their complexions look natural.
- 3-D movies became popular in the 1950s. Audiences had to wear special glasses to get the 3-D effect.

INDEX

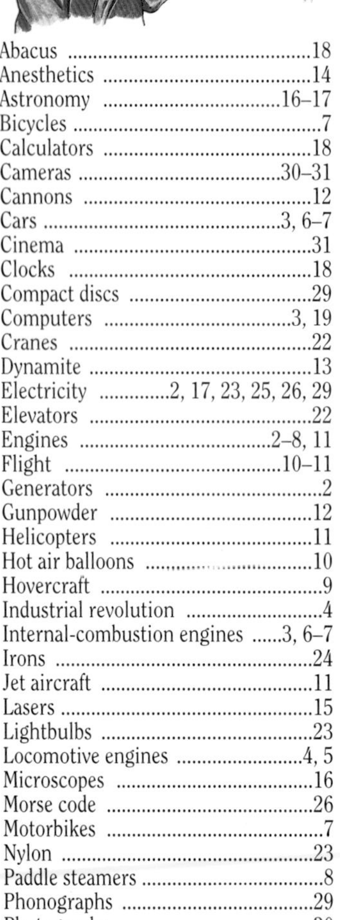

Published in 1997 by Creative Education
123 South Broad Street
Mankato, Minnesota 56001
Creative Education is an imprint
of The Creative Company
Written by Jilly MacLeod
Designed by Jane Molineaux
Cover design by Eric Madsen
Illustrations by Julian Baker, Charlotte Hard
and Kevin Maddison
Photographs by Image Select and Ann Ronan
of Image Select

4' ad

Printed and bound in Hong Kong.

**Library of Congress
Cataloging-in-Publication Data**
MacLeod, Jilly.
Great inventions / by Jilly MacLeod.
p. cm. - (It's a fact!)
Includes index.
Summary: Presents unusual facts about inventions over the centuries.
ISBN 0-88682-860-0

1. Inventions-History-Miscellanea-Juvenile literature. [1. Inventions-History-Miscellanea.]
I. Title. II. Series.
T15.M34 1997 96-35296
609-dc20
EDCBA